Peter and the Wolf

A SIENA BOOK

Siena is an imprint of Parragon Books

Published by Parragon Book Service Ltd.
Units 13-17, Avonbridge Trading Estate,
Atlantic Road, Avonmouth, Bristol BS11 9QD

Produced by The Templar Company plc, Pippbrook Mill,
London Road, Dorking, Surrey RH4 1JE

Designed by Mark Kingsley-Monks

Printed and bound in Italy
ISBN 0-75251-296-X

Peter and the Wolf

Illustrated by Carole Sharpe
Retold by Dugald Steer

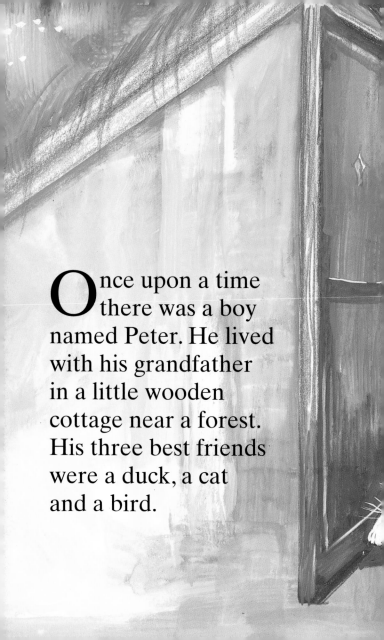

Once upon a time there was a boy named Peter. He lived with his grandfather in a little wooden cottage near a forest. His three best friends were a duck, a cat and a bird.

The duck lived in the duckpond that was near Peter's garden. She loved to keep Peter company as he sat and fished in the pond.

The cat liked being indoors. She loved to play games with Peter and together they spent hours chasing after marbles

and trying to catch spinning tops. When Peter was busy, the cat would just curl up and sleep by the warm stove.

The bird woke Peter each morning with her chirruping, and he would run out into the garden to find her.

"Do not go further than the meadow!" his grandfather would call after him. "There are wolves in the forest!"

Sadly however, Peter's three friends did not like each other.

One day Peter went down to the pond and the bird began to tease the duck terribly, flying round her head and calling her names.

The cat nearly caught the bird, which flew up into a tree to safety. The cat began climbing the tree, but the bird was well out of reach.

Just then, a wolf ran out of the forest. In no time at all he had gobbled up the duck!

Peter ran back to the garden and shut the gate behind him.

The wolf looked up at
the cat and the bird and
licked his lips. Peter wished
he could help them. Then he
had an idea. He fetched a
rope and climbed into the
tree from the garden wall.

"Little bird," said Peter,
when he had climbed the tree.
"Fly down and circle around
the wolf's nose."

The little bird was scared at
first, but she soon began to
enjoy teasing the wolf. How
she annoyed him!

The angry wolf was so busy snapping and growling at the bird that he did not see Peter lowering a loop of rope. Suddenly his tail flicked inside the loop, and Peter pulled the rope tight. The wolf was caught!

Just then, some hunters
came by. They had been
tracking the wolf through the
forest all day.

They tied the wolf up and took him to the zoo, with the duck still quack, quacking away inside his tummy!

Titles in this series include: